The Wizard OF OZ

This edition first published in the UK in 2008 by Green Umbrella Publishing for Pinnacle Vision

Publisher Alan Jones, Design and artwork by David Wildish, Creative Director Kevin Gardner

Printed and bound in China, ISBN 978-1-906554-04-0

Twelve-year-old Dorothy lives in Kansas with her Auntie Anne and Uncle Henry and her little dog, Toto. One day there is a very strong tornado heading for the house. Auntie Anne manages to escape as does Uncle Henry, but when Dorothy arrives at the house in the strong wind she finds that she and Toto are being carried away by the storm. The house comes to rest in a place that Dorothy does not recognise. She is in Munchkin Land and is greeted by the Good Witch of the North.

The witch thanks Dorothy for all she has done to destroy the Wicked Witch of the East. "But, I didn't do anything!" says Dorothy.

The Good Witch
points to the house
and tells the little
girl that it landed
on the Evil Witch. Dorothy can see the Witch's
feet sticking out from below the wooden house.
All the little girl wants is to go home.

The Good Witch gives Dorothy a pair of silver slippers and plants a kiss on her forehead. This gives her the mark of the Good Witch and means that she will be safe wherever she goes. Next, the Good Witch of the North tells Dorothy to take Toto and head for the Emerald City where she will find the Wizard of Oz.

He will be able to help she tells her, but she warns Dorothy to stick to the yellow road which will lead her right to the city. As Dorothy begins her journey she meets a Scarecrow who can talk. The Scarecrow is lovely but says he has no brain. Dorothy invites him to come along to the Emerald City to see if the Wizard can give him the brain he desires.

As the two make their way along the road it begins to rain and they seek refuge in a house where there is no one home. When the rain passes they set out again and hear a strange noise. They come across a Tin Man who is unable to move. He asks them kindly if they will fetch some oil from his house as the rain has made him all rusty. As soon as he is mended, the Tin Man explains that the Wicked Witch put a curse on him and changed him from being a man into a creature made of tin.

He also has no heart and Dorothy invites him to join them to see the Wizard. She believes that he may be able to give the Tin Man a heart.

A little further on the three are attacked by a big fierce Lion. Except the Lion isn't fierce at all. In fact, he has no courage. Dorothy thinks it would be a good idea for the Lion to join them. Perhaps the Wizard could give him some courage.

But, then the four new friends hear the menacing sound of the Caladaz, fearsome creatures with faces like tigers and bodies like bears.

They manage to escape by jumping a wide
cavern and they finish their journey to the
Emerald City. They soon find the Wizard of Oz
who says he will grant all their wishes as long as
they defeat the Wicked Witch of the West first.

The friends agree and soon find themselves under attack from some Winkeys who are slaves of the Wicked

Witch. They escape from the Winkeys and spy the Witch's castle, but they are soon picked up by the Evil Witch's Flying Monkeys.

Once trapped inside the castle, the four friends all fall foul of the Witch. Scarecrow has his stuffing knocked out of him and Dorothy is forced to clean the floor.

Toto attacks the Witch's umbrella when she points it too closely at Dorothy. The Witch tries to hit out at the little dog which makes Dorothy very angry. She throws her bucket of water over the Witch and she starts to melt.

Dorothy had not meant to hurt the Witch but it seems that water was all that was needed to destroy her. Once free from the Witch, the flying monkeys thank Dorothy and tell her she has three requests that she can make of them.

The first thing she asks for is for them to take her
and her friends back to the Emerald City.
They face the Wizard once again but he refuses
to carry out their wishes.

Dorothy tells the Wizard he is no Wizard if he cannot help them and a man comes from behind the screen to reveal that Dorothy is right.

He landed in Munchkin Land
in a balloon so the people
thought he was a Wizard.
He had not been able to leave
because of the two Evil Witches. Before he goes,
the Wizard tells the Scarecrow that he has had
some good ideas and gives him his glasses.

He does have a brain. He tells Lion that he is very brave and he does have courage and he gives the Tin Man a little red heart to show him that he has had a heart all along. As he leaves in his hot air balloon he tells Dorothy to seek help from Glinda, the Good Witch of the South.

Scarecrow suggests they ask the Flying Monkeys to take Dorothy home, but they cannot carry out the request as they are unable to fly all that way. But, they can take her to see Glinda.

The Good Witch tells Dorothy that she had the power within her slippers all along. "Close your eyes and click your heels together three times," she tells the young girl.

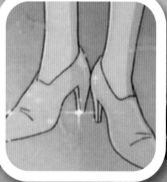